Hello, Family Members,

Learning to read is one of the most important accomplishments of early childhood. **Hello Reader!** books are designed to help children become skilled readers who like to read. Beginning readers learn to read by remembering frequently used words like "the," "is," and "and"; by using phonics skills to decode new words; and by interpreting picture and text clues. These books provide both the stories children enjoy and the structure they need to read fluently and independently. Here are suggestions for helping your child *before, during,* and *after* reading:

Before

- Look at the cover and pictures and have your child predict what the story is about.
- Read the story to your child.
- Encourage your child to chime in with familiar words and phrases.
- Echo read with your child by reading a line first and having your child read it after you do.

During

- Have your child think about a word he or she does not recognize right away. Provide hints such as "Let's see if we know the sounds" and "Have we read other words like this one?"
- Encourage your child to use phonics skills to sound out new words.
- Provide the word for your child when more assistance is needed so that he or she does not struggle and the experience of reading with you is a positive one.
- Encourage your child to have fun by reading with a lot of expression . . . like an actor!

After

- Have your child keep lists of interesting and favorite words.
- Encourage your child to read the books over and over again. Have him or her read to brothers, sisters, grandparents, and even teddy bears. Repeated readings develop confidence in young readers.
- Talk about the stories. Ask and answer questions. Share ideas about the funniest and most interesting characters and events in the stories.

I do hope that you and your child enjoy this book.

—Francie Alexander
Reading Specialist,
Scholastic's Learning Ventures

To each other

**Go to www.scholastic.com for web site information
on Scholastic authors and illustrators.**

Text copyright © 2001 by Daniel Pinkwater.
Illustrations copyright © 2001 by Jill Pinkwater.
All rights reserved. Published by Scholastic Inc.
SCHOLASTIC, HELLO READER, CARTWHEEL BOOKS, and associated logos
are trademarks and/or registered trademarks of Scholastic Inc.

ISBN 0-439-21678-8

Library of Congress Cataloging-in-Publication Data available

10 9 8 7 6 5 4 3 2 1   01 02 03 04 05

Printed in the U.S.A.   24

First printing, May 2001

Cone Kong
The Scary Ice Cream Giant

by Daniel Pinkwater
Illustrated by Jill Pinkwater

Hello Reader! — Level 2

SCHOLASTIC INC.

Cartwheel
·B·O·O·K·S·®

New York   Toronto   London   Auckland   Sydney
Mexico City   New Delhi   Hong Kong

Captain Charles Handsome is famous for having adventures. This time he is taking his ship, the *Bouncing Betty Beautiful*, to spooky Gull Island.

The ship is named after his girlfriend, Bouncing Betty Beautiful, a pretty young walrus.

The simple islanders of Gull Island are all afraid of The Great Cone, an ice-cream cone of spectacular size.

Captain Charles Handsome is not afraid.
"I will capture this Cone," he says.
"Come, Bouncing Betty Beautiful.
Let us go into the jungle."

But Captain Charles Handsome
and his crew are afraid of Cone when
they meet him. They run away.

But Bouncing Betty Beautiful is not afraid.

"Look! He is a nice ice-cream cone!" Bouncing Betty Beautiful says.

The Great Cone picks her up
and is about to run deeper into
the jungle with her.

But Captain Charles Handsome and his crew come back. They spray Cone with whipped cream. This confuses the gigantic wild ice-cream cone, and they are able to tie him with ropes.

When the *Bouncing Betty Beautiful* steams into the harbor, the people of the Big City crowd around to see.

"Look! Captain Charles Handsome has gone on another adventure and brought back a giant wild beast. What do you call him, Captain?"

"I call him Cone Kong," Captain Charles Handsome says. "Come to the Ice Palace Theater on Tuesday. I will show him to everyone."

The newspapers have headlines:
ADVENTURER CAPTURES
GIANT ICE-CREAM CONE.
WILL SHOW HIM AT ICE PALACE
THEATER ON TUESDAY!

The people of the Big City talk of nothing but the great beast ice-cream cone and can hardly wait for Tuesday.

Tuesday night comes! Everyone goes to the Ice Palace Theater.

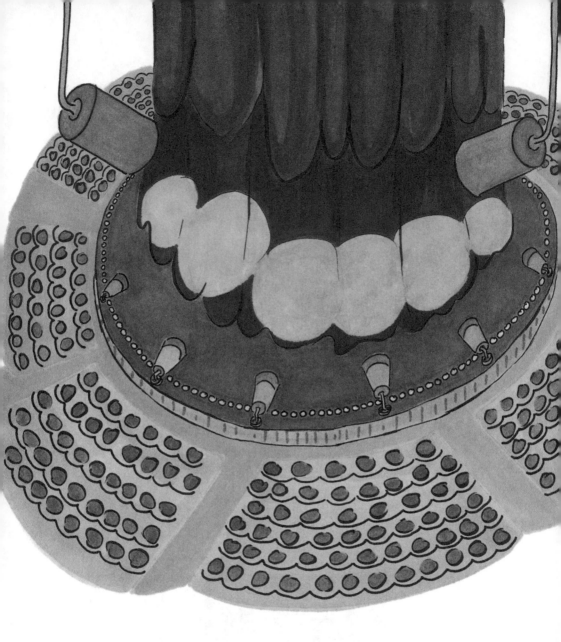

There are bright lights. Bands are playing. People are eating popcorn and stamping their feet.

Finally, the curtains open. Cone
Kong is in chains. Captain Charles
Handsome stands before him.

"I present to you . . . Cone Kong!"
he says.

There are reporters.
"How did you catch him?"
"What flavor is he?"
"Why doesn't he melt?"
They shout their questions.

There are cameras. Bright lights
come on. People want pictures of
Cone. Cone does not like the lights.

"Please! Please! No lights!" Captain
Charles Handsome shouts.
But it is too late. Cone Kong
breaks his chains!

He is free! He is free!
Cone Kong runs out of the
theater and into the night.

Later, Bouncing Betty Beautiful is in her fancy apartment, talking to Captain Charles Handsome.

"So, where do you suppose Cone Kong went?" she asks.

Just then, Cone Kong appears at her window. He grabs Bouncing Betty Beautiful and carries her with him.

He is climbing the Igloo Tower,
the tallest building in the Big City.

Save her! Save Bouncing Betty Beautiful! The citizens of the Big City try to distract Cone Kong by throwing chocolate sprinkles and crushed peanuts at him.

At the very top of the Igloo Tower, Cone Kong carefully puts Bouncing Betty Beautiful down so he can fend off the sprinkles. But he loses his balance . . . he teeters . . . he falls!

Cone Kong is falling! Falling! Falling!
Will he go *Splot*? Will he go *Gloomph*?

No! He bounces! He bounces! He bounces down the street, he bounces onto the *Bouncing Betty Beautiful*, (not the walrus-girl . . . the ship), and sets sail for Gull Island.

Captain Charles Handsome watches his ship sail out of sight.

"Cone Kong has escaped," he says. "The biggest ice-cream cone ever known. We never even learned what flavor he was."

"It was bouncing that saved the beast."